EASY UPCYCLED CRAFTS

# "GLASS JAR"

## CRAFTS

BY BETSY RATHBURN

Express!

BELLWETHER MEDIA · MINNEAPOLIS, MN

# Express!

Imagination comes alive in **Express!** Transform the everyday into the fresh and new, discover ways to stir up flavor and excitement, and experiment with new ideas and materials. Express! makerspace books: where your next creative adventure begins!

This edition first published in 2022 by Bellwether Media, Inc.

No part of this publication may be reproduced in whole or in part without written permission of the publisher. For information regarding permission, write to Bellwether Media, Inc., Attention: Permissions Department, 6012 Blue Circle Drive, Minnetonka, MN 55343.

Library of Congress Cataloging-in-Publication Data

Names: Rathburn, Betsy, author.
Title: Glass jar crafts / by Betsy Rathburn.
Description: Minneapolis, MN : Bellwether Media, Inc., 2022. | Series: Express! : Easy upcycled crafts |
    Includes bibliographical references and index. | Audience: Ages 7-13 | Audience: Grades 4-6 |
    Summary: "Information accompanies step-by-step instructions on how to upcycle glass jars into fun crafts.
    The text level and subject matter are intended for students in grades 3 through 8"-- Provided by publisher.
Identifiers: LCCN 2021049544 (print) | LCCN 2021049545 (ebook) | ISBN 9781644876411 (library binding) |
    ISBN 9781648346521 (ebook)
Subjects: LCSH: Glass craft--Juvenile literature. | Glass jars--Recycling--Juvenile literature.
Classification: LCC TT298 .R37 2022  (print) | LCC TT298  (ebook) | DDC 748.5028/4--dc23/eng/20211028
LC record available at https://lccn.loc.gov/2021049544
LC ebook record available at https://lccn.loc.gov/2021049545

Text copyright © 2022 by Bellwether Media, Inc. EXPRESS and associated logos are trademarks and/or registered trademarks of Bellwether Media, Inc.

Editor: Rebecca Sabelko
Series Design: Jeffrey Kollock
Book Designer: Laura Sowers
Craft model making and photography: Jessica Moon
Craft instructions: Jennifer Sanderson

Printed in the United States of America, North Mankato, MN.

# TABLE OF CONTENTS

# FROM TRASH TO TREASURE

Upcycling involves creatively reusing trash and other unwanted materials. It is the process of turning waste into something new that has value. Waste materials can be anything found in the recycling, from cardboard boxes and egg cartons to glass jars, plastic bottles, and even old art supplies!

One of the best things about upcycling is that it reduces the amount of trash that goes into **landfills**, which helps the **environment**. Upcycling is also an affordable way to create art.

In this book, you will use glass jars to make bright, fun craft projects. Use what you have and have a great time!

! Top Tip

Look for this feature throughout the book. It will give you tips that will help improve your projects.

# MATERIALS AND TOOLS

To make these projects, you will need glass jars of different shapes and sizes. Remove the labels from old pasta, jelly, and pickle jars. Clean them out and use them to make crafts!

## You will also need

- glue
- scissors
- paintbrushes
- paints

# COIN BANK

**Extra materials needed**
- glass jar with plastic lid
- ribbon
- bow or extra ribbon

Saving money is important! It helps people buy expensive items or get items they need in **emergencies**. Some people **invest** money they save. They buy **stocks** or earn **interest** from banks.

This coin bank will give you a good place to keep money. What will you save up for?

**1**

Paint the outside of the jar and let it dry.

**2**

Use different colors to paint the bottom half of the jar. Add polka dots, stripes, or another fun pattern. Let it dry.

## 3

Wrap the ribbon around the jar and cut it to size. Then, glue it around the jar. Glue the bow to the front.

## 4

Have an adult cut a coin slot in the top of the lid, then paint the lid to match the jar. Your coin bank is complete!

cut

### ! Top Tip

Make the coin slot long enough to fit different coins. Test the coin slot with the biggest coin you have. Make it bigger if needed.

**FINAL**

# WASHI TAPE VASE

**Extra materials needed**
- large glass bottle or jar
- washi tape
- yarn
- flowers

Washi tape is a type of reusable tape. Once you stick it, you can peel it off and stick it again! Its name comes from washi paper. This type of Japanese paper dates back more than 1,000 years.

Today, washi tape comes in many colors and patterns. People use it to make crafts. Try using washi tape to upcycle an old bottle or jar into a colorful vase!

**1**

Plan out how you will decorate the bottle or jar. Arrange the rolls of washi tape to follow the pattern you created.

**2**

Wrap a piece of washi tape around the outside of the jar. Continue adding washi tape until your design is complete.

8

**3**

Wrap washi tape around the rim of the jar. Tie the yarn over the washi tape on the rim to complete the vase. Fill the vase with water and place the flowers inside!

**! Top Tip**

To easily remove the labels from your bottles or jars, soak them in warm, soapy water. Use a tough scrubber to remove any remaining glue.

**FINAL**

9

# PHOTO HOLDER

**Extra materials needed**
- glass jar
- pebbles or sand
- seashells
- kitchen tongs
- ribbon
- craft stick
- photograph

The world's first photograph was taken in 1826! This black-and-white picture shows the view outside a window in France. Today, better cameras and color film let us take better quality photos. Camera phones let us take and send photos quickly.

This craft will show you how to make a **unique** display for your photos. What picture will you put inside?

**1**

Fill the bottom of the glass jar about one-fourth of the way full with pebbles or sand.

**2**

Place seashells on top of the pebbles or sand. Use kitchen tongs to help place the seashells where you want them.

**!** **Top Tip**

If you do not have seashells, decorate your photo holder with your favorite small toys or cool rocks!

**3**

Cut the piece of ribbon to fit around the rim of the jar and glue it in place.

**4**

Cut the photograph to fit inside the jar. Glue the craft stick to the back of the photo. Then, put the photo inside the jar, using the pebbles or sand to hold the craft stick in place. Your photo display is complete!

**glue**

**FINAL**

# SUCCULENT PLANTER

**Succulents** are plants that grow in dry places. When it rains, the plants store water in their stems, roots, and thick leaves. They survive until the next rainfall!

Succulents are easy to grow at home. Make a planter from a glass jar. Then, add soil and plant the succulent. Only water the plant when the soil is completely dry!

## 1

Gather large bunches of yarn in each color. Fill a plastic container with glue. Soak one bunch of yarn in the glue.

**make sure all of the yarn is covered**

## 2

When the yarn is soaked through, carefully wrap it around the bottom half of the jar. Squeeze any extra glue from the yarn as you do this.

## 3

Thoroughly soak the second bunch of yarn in glue. Then, wrap it around the top of the jar. Squeeze out any extra glue as you do this. The jar should be completely covered in yarn.

## 4

Thoroughly soak the third bunch of yarn in glue. Then, wrap it around the middle of the jar where the previous two bunches meet. Squeeze out any extra glue as you do this. Let the yarn dry completely. Then, fill the jar with soil and plant the succulent!

### ! Top Tip

Succulents grow best in places with plenty of sunlight. Place your planter near a sunny window and watch your succulent grow!

**FINAL**

13

# CANDLE HOLDER

**Extra materials needed**
- shallow glass jar
- colorful tissue paper
- real or battery-operated tea light candle

The earliest candles were made from plant parts and animal fat. These were called rushlights. Later, people made **wicks** by dipping rolled paper into melted **tallow** or beeswax. The candles were lit to bring light and to decorate celebrations.

This candle holder can easily be made from a glass jar. You can use a real candle or a battery-operated candle.

**1**

Rip the tissue paper into small pieces. Working in sections, use a paintbrush to cover the outside of the glass jar with glue. Stick on pieces of tissue paper and let them dry. Continue until the entire jar is covered. Let it dry.

14

## 2

Repeat Step 1 to add another layer of tissue paper, covering any gaps. Let it dry.

make sure all the gaps are covered

## 3

Add a third layer of tissue paper. When the paper is dry, light the tea light candle and place it in the jar.

## ! Top Tip

If you do not have tissue paper, try using old gift wrap. The thinner the paper, the better the light will shine through the jar.

FINAL

# PASTA VASE

Pasta is one of the most popular foods in the world! There are many different types of pasta. Ravioli are pockets stuffed with meat or cheese. Penne is shaped like a **cylinder** to better hold sauces.

This craft will let you use pasta in a new way. Cover a glass jar in your favorite pasta shapes to make a vase!

**1**

Gather several pastas of different shapes and paint them bright colors.

**2**

Plan out how you will decorate the vase. Design a fun pattern with different shapes and colors. Then, glue the pasta to the outside of the glass jar to make the pattern.

glue

16

## 3

Fill the jar halfway with water. Then, place cut flowers in the jar. Display your pasta vase!

### ! Top Tip

To easily paint the pasta, spread it out in a single layer. Paint one side first and let it dry. Then, flip the pasta over to paint the other side.

**FINAL**

17

# SNOW GLOBE

**Extra materials needed**
- glass jar with lid
- cotton balls
- old toys or figures
- string
- silver star sequins
- ribbon

Snow globes are glass containers that hold **models** of cities, nature, and other scenes. When you shake them, it looks like it is snowing! Many people collect snow globes. The world's largest collection has more than 4,000 snow globes!

With glass jars and old toys, you can make your own snow globe collection!

**1**

To make snow, pull apart several cotton balls. Place them in the bottom of the jar.

**2**

Carefully place the toys or figures on top of the cotton balls to make a scene.

## 3

Cut the string into different lengths. Make sure they are all shorter than the length of the jar. Glue the sequins onto the ends of the strings. Then, glue the other ends onto the inside of the jar lid.

glue

## 4

Put the lid on the jar so that the sequins hang down into the jar. Finish the snow globe by decorating the rim of the jar with ribbon.

## ! Top Tip

Before you put the lid on your snow globe, try adding glitter. It will sparkle like fresh snow!

**FINAL**

# REINDEER MUG

**Extra materials needed**
- glass jar mug with lid and handle
- plain brown or tan fabric
- large red pom-pom
- googly eyes
- black pipe cleaners

Cartoon reindeer, like Rudolph, are popular characters. But reindeer are real animals. Also called caribou, they are known for their big **antlers**. They eat **lichens** that grow in the cold regions where they live.

Follow this craft to make a fun reindeer mug. Fill it with treats and give it as a gift!

## 1

Measure the fabric so that it is long enough to go around the jar and narrow enough to go through the handle. Cut it to size, then glue it in place.

## 2

Glue the red pom-pom to the middle of the fabric on the front of the mug.

20

## 3

Glue the googly eyes above the red pom-pom.

## 4

Twist and bend the pipe cleaners to make reindeer antlers. Wrap them around the rim of the jar and twist them in place. Fill the jar with treats. Enjoy the treat mug now or give it as a gift!

**FINAL**

**! Top Tip**

Try making other glass mug animals! To make a rabbit, use small black pom-poms for the nose and tail. Bend pipe cleaners to make the ears.

21

# GLOSSARY

**antlers**—branched bones on the heads of some animals; antlers look like horns.

**cylinder**—a three-dimensional shape with straight sides and round openings on either end

**emergencies**—unexpected situations that require immediate action

**environment**—the natural world

**interest**—money paid in exchange for the use of borrowed money; interest is usually a percentage of the amount borrowed.

**invest**—to give money to a person or business in order to make more money later

**landfills**—places where waste is dumped and buried

**lichens**—plantlike living things that grow on rocks

**models**—small copies of things

**stocks**—shares in the value of a company, which can be bought, sold, or traded; people invest in stocks to earn money from them.

**succulents**—plants with fleshy leaves that hold water

**tallow**—solid animal fat that can be used to make soap, candles, and other items

**unique**—one of a kind

**wicks**—strings or pieces of material in candles or lamps that are lit for burning

# TO LEARN MORE

## AT THE LIBRARY

Labrecque, Ellen. *Recycling and Waste*. Ann Arbor, Mich.: Cherry Lake Publishing, 2018.

Priddy, Brenda. *The Mason Jar Scientist: 30 Jarring STEAM-Based Projects*. New York, N.Y.: Racehorse for Young Readers, 2018.

Wood, Alix. *Mason Jar Creations*. New York, N.Y.: PowerKids Press, 2020.

## ON THE WEB

# FACTSURFER

Factsurfer.com gives you a safe, fun way to find more information.

1. Go to www.factsurfer.com.

2. Enter "glass jar crafts" into the search box and click 🔍.

3. Select your book cover to see a list of related content.

23

# INDEX

The images in this book are reproduced through the courtesy of: Gevorg Simonyan, p. 5 (glue); Kozak Sergii, p. 5 (scissors); Mouse family, p. 5 (bottom right); all other photos courtesy of Calcium.